To my father

~S.V.

The Rose's Smile

· Farizad of the Arabian Nights ·

David Kherdian

With pictures by Stefano Vitale

Henry Holt and Company

New York

Henry Holt and Company, Inc.
Publishers since 1866
115 West 18th Street
New York, New York 10011
Henry Holt is a registered trademark of Henry Holt and Company, Inc.

Published in Canada by Fitzhenry & Whiteside Ltd.,
195 Allstate Parkway, Markham, Ontario L3R 4T8.

Library of Congress Cataloging-in-Publication Data
Kherdian, David.
The rose's smile: Farizad of the Arabian nights /
David Kherdian; illustrated by Stefano Vitale.

Summary: Only the courage of the beautiful Farizad is able to
bring happiness out of the evil deeds of her mother's two jealous
older sisters.

[1. Fairy tales.   2. Arabs–Folklore.   3. Folklore–Arab countries.]
I. Vitale, Stefano, ill.   II. Arabian nights. English.   III. Title.
PZ8.K523Ro   1997   398.2'09538'02–dc21   96-52539

ISBN 0-8050-3912-0
First Edition--1997
Typography by Martha Rago
Printed in the United States of America on acid-free paper. ∞
1   3   5   7   9   10   8   6   4   2

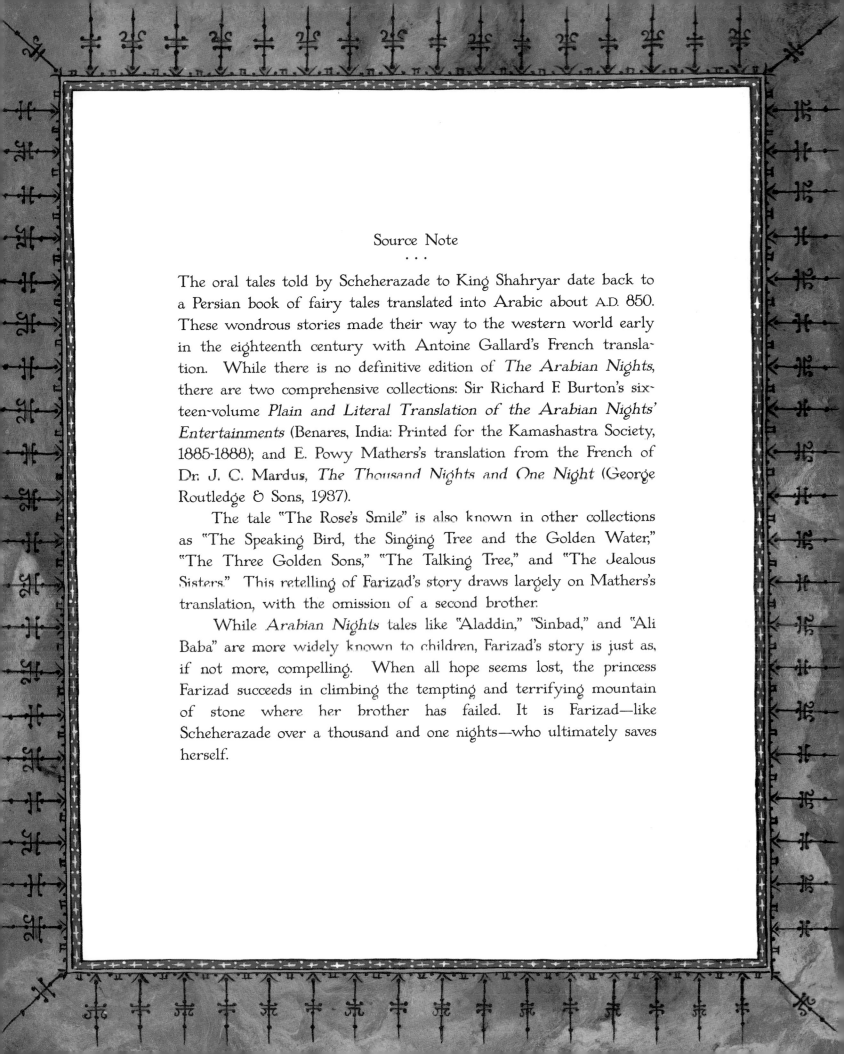

Source Note
· · ·

The oral tales told by Scheherazade to King Shahryar date back to a Persian book of fairy tales translated into Arabic about A.D. 850. These wondrous stories made their way to the western world early in the eighteenth century with Antoine Gallard's French translation. While there is no definitive edition of *The Arabian Nights*, there are two comprehensive collections: Sir Richard F. Burton's sixteen-volume *Plain and Literal Translation of the Arabian Nights' Entertainments* (Benares, India: Printed for the Kamashastra Society, 1885-1888); and E. Powy Mathers's translation from the French of Dr. J. C. Mardus, *The Thousand Nights and One Night* (George Routledge & Sons, 1987).

The tale "The Rose's Smile" is also known in other collections as "The Speaking Bird, the Singing Tree and the Golden Water," "The Three Golden Sons," "The Talking Tree," and "The Jealous Sisters." This retelling of Farizad's story draws largely on Mathers's translation, with the omission of a second brother.

While *Arabian Nights* tales like "Aladdin," "Sinbad," and "Ali Baba" are more widely known to children, Farizad's story is just as, if not more, compelling. When all hope seems lost, the princess Farizad succeeds in climbing the tempting and terrifying mountain of stone where her brother has failed. It is Farizad—like Scheherazade over a thousand and one nights—who ultimately saves herself.

Once, long ago in the far-off land of Arabia, there lived a benevolent young Sultan who was as handsome as he was kind. He loved the rich and the poor of his kingdom alike and often wandered in disguise through the streets of the poor to study their lives and to learn of their needs.

One evening, while the Sultan was passing through the poorest section of the city, he heard whisperings from a courtyard window. He concealed himself and eavesdropped on a conversation among three young maidens.

The oldest girl was saying, "I wish that I could marry the Sultan's pastry cook. You know how I love sweets. Then I could have for myself the finest pastries in the land, instead of the plain and meager food we now get to eat."

The second sister said, "Well, since we are talking about wishes that lead to marriage, I would like to marry the Sultan's own cook, the greatest chef in the land. Then I would be assured of being well fed for the rest of my days."

The two maidens turned and said to their younger sister, who until now had listened in silence, "And how about you, quiet one, don't you have a wish?"

The youngest of the sisters lowered her eyes and refused to speak. But her older sisters teased her until she finally admitted that she, too, had a wish. As she began speaking, her cheeks turned to rose and the Sultan thought to himself that her voice was like music. "It is my wish to marry the Sultan himself," she answered. "In time we would have a fine son, and then we would have a daughter whose hair would be made of gold and silver, while her tears, when she wept, would turn to pearls. Upon her lips would be the smile of the rose, and my Sultan would be so proud."

When the sisters laughed at her, she bowed her head once again and closed her lips. But destiny would soon reveal itself, for when the Sultan heard of the maidens' wishes, he knew at once that he would grant all of them. And not only for their sakes but for his own, because his own heart had already been opened to the youngest of the maidens.

The next morning he sent for the three sisters. They trembled as they stood in his presence and awaited his command. But they had no reason to be frightened. First he told the two eldest sisters that their wishes would be fulfilled. Then he beckoned the youngest of the maidens to come sit beside him on the throne. "And you will be my Queen," he said.

The wedding for the three couples took place that very day. But the older sisters, instead of being happy at having their wishes answered, were wound tight in the grip of jealousy. They could no longer endure the beauty of the youngest, nor could they accept the splendor that surrounded her. The day had not darkened before they began to plot against her.

At the end of nine months the young Queen had a son who was as beautiful as the crescent of the new moon. But her bitter sisters, who were the attending midwives, put the infant in a willow basket and set it afloat on a stream at the edge of the palace. In the crib they quickly substituted a dead dog for the baby before either parent had had a chance to see the infant.

The next day, when the Sultan and the Queen visited their child, they were so overcome with grief that they shut themselves deep inside the palace walls, where they shrouded their lives in darkness.

The chief gardener of the palace was thinning some new growth near the stream that same day when he found the baby. Since he and his wife were childless, he took this as a gift from Allah, and rushed home to his wife with the beautiful infant. They called the boy Farid.

A year later, the Queen was to give birth again, and now her sisters, whose jealousy only increased with time, put a dead mouse in the baby's place. They set the child in a willow basket on the same stream and the child was found by the same kind gardener. This time he and his wife enjoyed the blessings of a little girl whom they named Farizad.

The Sultan felt cursed by a marriage that would produce dead animals instead of children. Although he loved his wife, he had her put away in a separate chamber of the palace. The Queen was left to live alone with her sorrow, while her heartless sisters rejoiced in her suffering.

The years passed, and the children grew in beauty, kindness, and wisdom, while their adopted parents grew old. Finally, the time came for the gardener to retire, and the kind Sultan offered him a beautiful home of his own at the edge of the palace grounds, with magnificent gardens that had been laid out long ago by the old gardener himself. In time the old couple died and the secret of their two children was buried with them.

One day while Farizad was alone in the garden, an old woman appeared and asked if she could rest there awhile. The kind Farizad led her to a shady glen and offered her refreshments. When the old woman recovered from her apparent weariness, she told Farizad that this garden was a place of beauty unlike anything that had ever been seen before. "However," she said to Farizad, "the garden lacks three things which you must find before its unsurpassed beauty will be complete."

"I beg you, Good Mother," said Farizad, "tell me what those three things might be."

"I will tell you as a reward for your kindness to me," the old woman said. "The first thing you must do is to find Bulbul al-Hazar, the Talking Bird.

"The second thing you must seek and find is the Singing Tree.

"And the third thing you must possess is the Water of Gold. Only when these three marvels are in your garden will your destiny be complete. All three lie somewhere beyond Kaf Mountain. You can find the path just behind the gardens here. After you follow where it leads for twenty days, someone will direct you the rest of the way." And with her final words uttered, the old woman disappeared.

Farizad was convinced that what the old woman said was true, and that she could not continue her life without obtaining these treasures.

Farizad wept as she wandered through the gardens, leaving a long trail of pearls behind her.

When her brother returned from his hunting trip, he followed the pearls to his grieving sister. When he asked her what had happened, Farizad told him about the old woman and how she had been admonished to find the Talking Bird, the Singing Tree, and the Water of Gold.

Farid put his arm around his sister's shoulder and said, "Calm yourself, sweet sister, as you can see my horse is still saddled. I will go immediately to find these three marvels for our garden." He embraced Farizad and gave her a knife, the handle of which was encrusted with the pearls of Farizad's earliest tears. "From time to time," he advised her, "check the blade of this knife. If it loses its luster, you will know that I am in trouble. And if it appears to have blood on it, you will know that my life has ended, and you will then be responsible for your own needs." Before she could protest, Farid mounted his horse and hurried onto the path.

After twenty days and nights, Farid finally came upon an old man sitting beside the path. His hair was so long that it completely covered his face. His beard grew down to his toes and his nails were almost as long as his hands. Who could say how long he had been sitting there?

Farid called to him but he did not respond. Farid dismounted and took a pair of scissors from his saddlebag. He trimmed the old man's hair so he could see, and cut his beard and his mustache. Then he carefully cut all the nails of his hands and feet.

When he was done, the old man smiled.

Farid said, "Old man, will you tell me how I can find the Talking Bird, the Singing Tree, and the Water of Gold?"

The old man did not hesitate. "Because of your kindness, I will tell you. But I must warn you, the way is dangerous and not one single traveler has returned from that place."

He gave Farid a ball of red granite. "Throw the ball ahead of you," he said, "and it will guide you. When it stops rolling, secure your horse's bridle to the ball of granite and climb the mountain. It is very dangerous and you must not listen to voices, but keep your attention on your quest. When you reach the summit, you will find Bulbul al-Hazar, the Talking Bird, and he will lead you to the Singing Tree and the Water of Gold. May Allah grace you with success."

Farid jumped on his horse and followed the old man's directions. When the granite ball stopped at the base of a mountain, he tethered his horse to the ball and began his ascent. As he climbed the mountain he worked to keep his attention on his footing and his quest. He heard many voices but he stayed with the instructions he had been given, and tried not to notice the masses of black stones about him that resembled human forms. Suddenly he heard a blood-curdling cry and in spite of himself he turned. And in his turning he, too, was changed into a mass of black stone.

At that moment Farizad picked up the knife her brother had given her, and saw that it had lost its shine. "Oh, Farid," she cried. "My dear brother has come to harm. I must go quickly to save him."

Farizad set out on her journey and on the twentieth day she, too, met the old man, who tried to turn her from her path. But when he saw that her mind was set, he gave her two wisps of cotton to tuck into her ears.

Farizad followed the red granite ball as her brother before her had done, and she climbed the mountain that made the terrible sounds, but she could only hear a vague humming. She climbed on until at last she reached the top of the mountain, and there on the summit was Bulbul al-Hazar, the Talking Bird, in a golden cage on a golden pedestal. "At last you are mine, Talking Bird!" she exclaimed. She pulled the cotton from her ears, for the voices around her had now been stilled. When she heard the Talking Bird speak, she forgot her weariness.

With Bulbul's help she found the Singing Tree and listened to the beautiful singing of its leaves. She plucked the tiniest branch to plant in her garden.

Once again Bulbul guided her, leading her to look behind a secret blue stone, and there she found the Water of Gold. She filled a small urn that seemed to have been placed there for her need.

"O most beautiful Bulbul al-Hazar," she cried, "I have one more wish, and that is to free my brother."

Bulbul al-Hazar sweetly sang her answer, and Farizad descended the mountain sprinkling the Water of Gold on each black stone she saw. With each sprinkling a man emerged, transformed from out of the stone, and among them was her brother, Farid.

Farizad, in the company of the men she had freed, returned to where the old man had sat to thank him, but his work was done and he had disappeared. So they traveled on, with each of the freed men departing one by one to their separate lands. And then, on the twentieth day, Farid and Farizad arrived at their home.

Farizad went to work at once on her garden. She hung the cage of Bulbul in the Jasmine Arbor, where with his beautiful voice he attracted all the birds of the garden in chorus. She planted the cutting from the Singing Tree with great care, and before the day had elapsed it grew into a tree as beautiful as the one it had come from. Then she poured the last of the Water of Gold into the alabaster basin of the fountain. The gold droplet spread and gave birth to golden sprays that rippled outward beyond forever. She knew that she had done what was needed, even though she could not say with her mind what that was. But in her heart she was happy and fulfilled and knew that the meaning of her actions would soon be revealed to her.

The next day, while Farid was hunting, he met the Sultan walking on his path. Farid dismounted to pay him homage. The Sultan felt himself drawn at once to the handsome youth and began speaking to him. It soon transpired that he learned that Farid and his sister were his old gardener's children. He invited himself to their home for a visit.

At Bulbul's odd request Farizad asked the cook to prepare a dish of cucumbers stuffed with pearls to serve the Sultan. Then she covered her face with a veil and bowed to greet him. The Sultan was overwhelmed by the beauty of the garden, with its Singing Tree, Water of Gold, and of course the beautiful Talking Bird. But he was especially taken by the sweet grace of Farizad, who reminded him of the children he had long ago wished to have for himself and his Queen.

After he had relaxed for a while under the Jasmine Arbor and listened to the sweet sounds of Bulbul and the Singing Tree, he was served the cucumbers stuffed with pearls. He began to comment on the oddity of the dish, but Bulbul al-Hazar called out to him, "If you can believe that your Queen could give birth to animals, then how can you think it odd to eat pearls?"

Then Bulbul repeated the words the Queen had said on the night the Sultan had seen her for the first time. The Sultan wept as he heard again the loving description of the two children she claimed they would have. "Upon her lips would be the smile of the rose, and my Sultan would be so proud," Bulbul intoned in the voice of the Queen.

Bulbul raised his voice again. "Unveil yourself before your father, Farizad."

Farizad unveiled herself and her gold and silver hair fell down over her shoulders. "Behold your daughter, Sultan. The pearls of happiness are on her eyelids and on her lips the smile of the rose," Bulbul said. And before long the whole of the tale had been told and the Sultan and his two children embraced each other and wept with joy.

W hen they had calmed themselves and dried their tears, they rushed to the palace to release the Queen from her lonely sanctuary and into the joy and love of her family, who had at last been gathered into a single whole.

The evil sisters were turned to stone by their own rage, while the Sultan and his Queen, and of course their two devoted children, lived long and happy lives, as their destiny had determined and their fate ordained.